ZOOM *at* SEA

BY
TIM WYNNE-JONES

PICTURES BY
ERIC BEDDOWS

GROUNDWOOD BOOKS ⚓ HOUSE OF ANANSI PRESS

TORONTO   BERKELEY

Zoom loved water. Not to drink — he liked cream to drink — Zoom liked water to play with.

One night, when a leaky tap filled the kitchen sink, Zoom strapped wooden spoons to his feet with elastic bands and paddled in the water for hours. He loved it.

The next night he made a boat from a wicker basket with a towel for a sail. Blown around the bathtub all night, he was as happy as could be.

There was no stopping him. Every night when other self-respecting cats were out mousing and howling Zoom stayed indoors and sailed about in the dark. By day he watched the tap and dreamed.

One afternoon while dreaming in the attic he noticed a shelf he had not seen before. A dusty diary lay next to a photograph of a large yellow tomcat with white whiskers and a black sou'wester. It was inscribed: "For Zoom from Uncle Roy."

Zoom opened the diary and on the last page he found an address and a map. "The Sea and how to get there," it said.

The Sea was not far, really. Zoom took a bus. He arrived very early in the morning, at a house with a big front door. It was so early Zoom was afraid to knock but the light was on and if he listened closely he thought he could hear someone inside. With great excitement he rapped three times.

The door opened. Before him stood a large woman in a blue dress. She wore silver earrings and many silver bracelets on her wrists.

"I want to go to sea," said Zoom nervously.

The woman smiled, but said nothing. Zoom spoke louder.

"I'm Uncle Roy's nephew and I want to go to sea."

"Ahh!" said the woman, nodding her head. "Come in my little sailor."

Inside was cold and damp.

"I am Maria," said the woman. "I'm not ready just yet." The room was quiet and dark; everything was still. Far away Zoom could hear a sound like a leaky faucet.

He sat, trying to be patient, while Maria bustled around. Sometimes it was difficult to see her in the gloom, but he could hear the swish of her skirts and the tinkling of her bracelets.

The Sea was nothing like Uncle Roy had described in his diary. Zoom was sure he had made a mistake and he was just about to sneak away when Maria looked at her watch and winked.

"Now I'm ready."

And with that, she turned an enormous wheel several times to the right. The floor began to rumble and machinery began to whirr and hum. The room grew lighter and Zoom saw that it was very large.

Now Maria pushed a button and cranked a crank. Zoom could hear the sound of water rushing through the pipes. First there were only puddles but then it poured from the closets and lapped at his feet.

From rows upon rows of tiny doors Maria released sea gulls and sandpipers, pelicans and terns. From pots and cages she set free hundreds of crabs and octopi and squid who scurried this way and that across the sandy floor.

Maria laughed. Zoom laughed. This was more like it. Noise and sunlight and water, for now there was water everywhere.

Suddenly Zoom realized he could not even see the walls of this giant room. Only the sun coming up like gold, and silver fish dancing on the waves. Far away he could see a fishing boat.

Maria smiled and said, "Go on. It's all yours."

Quickly he gathered some old logs and laced them together with seaweed. He made a raft and decorated it with shells as white as Maria's teeth.

When it was ready, he pushed and he heaved with all his might and launched the raft into the waves.

"I'm at Sea!" he called.

He danced around on his driftwood deck and occasionally cupped his paws and shouted very loudly back to shore.

"More waves," or "More Sun," or "More fish."

Waves crashed against the raft. The sun beat down. Fish leaped across the bow and frolicked in his wake.

Zoom looked back toward the shore and saw Maria. He realized, then, that he was tired. The waves subsided and the water gently began to roll toward the shore. Zoom sat and let the tide drift him back.

He sat with Maria at her little table drinking tea and eating fish fritters and watched the sun sink into the sea. As the light dimmed, the room didn't seem half so big.

Maria's bun had come undone and there was sand in the ruffles at the bottom of her dress, but still she smiled and her jewelry tinkled silver in the twilight.

"Thank you for a great day," said Zoom as he stood at the door. "May I come back?"

"I'm sure you will," said Maria.

And he did.

Groundwood Books / House of Anansi Press
110 Spadina Avenue, Suite 801, Toronto, Ontario M5V 2K4
or c/o Publishers Group West
1700 Fourth Street, Berkeley, CA 94710

We acknowledge for their financial support of our publishing program the Canada Council for the Arts, the Government of Canada through the Canada Book Fund (CBF) and the Ontario Arts Council.

Library and Archives Canada Cataloguing in Publication
Wynne-Jones, Tim
Zoom at sea / written by Tim Wynne-Jones ;
illustrated by Eric Beddows.
Also issued in electronic format.
ISBN 978-1-55498-391-9
1. Cats—Juvenile fiction. I. Beddows, Eric II. Title.
PS8595.Y59Z6 2013   jC813'.54   C2013-900885-3

The illustrations were done in graphite pencil.
Design by Michael Solomon
Printed and bound in China

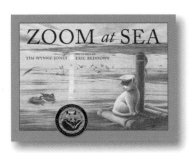

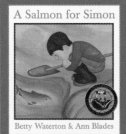